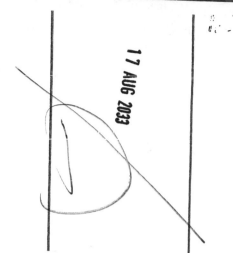

D0784578

EGMONT
We bring stories to life

First published in Great Britain in 2016
by Egmont UK Limited
The Yellow Building, 1 Nicholas Road, London W11 4AN

Thomas the Tank Engine & Friends™

CREATED BY BRITT ALLCROFT

HiT entertainment

ISBN 978 1 4052 7976 5
62417/003
Printed in Italy

Stay safe online. Egmont is not responsible for content hosted by third parties.

Written by Emily Stead. Designed by Claire Yeo.
Series designed by Martin Aggett.

Egmont takes its responsibility to the planet and its inhabitants very seriously.
We aim to use papers from well-managed forests run by responsible suppliers.

*This story is about James,
the Number 5 engine on The Fat
Controller's Railway. When he first
came to Sodor, all James thought
about was his shiny red paint, so
he soon got into trouble . . .*

James was a new engine with **shiny red paint**.

He had two small wheels in front and six big driving wheels behind.

"You can pull coaches or trucks," The Fat Controller told James. "You are a mixed-traffic engine."

James felt very proud.

One day James' job was to help Edward pull coaches.

"Be careful with your coaches, James," said Edward. "If you **BUMP** them they'll get cross!"

But James wasn't listening. All he was thinking about was his shiny red paint.

James and Edward brought the coaches to the platform. Some boys came to look at James.

"I'm such a **splendid engine**," thought James. He let out a big **WHEEEESH** of steam.

A shower of water fell on The Fat Controller. **Splash!** His new top hat was soaking wet!

James set off with his **wheels whirring**.

"Slow down, **James**!" old Edward called.

James was going so fast that at the next station, he steamed straight past the platform! They had to back up to let the passengers off.

"The Fat Controller won't be pleased," James sighed.

The next morning, The Fat Controller came to see James.

"If you don't behave better, I shall paint your **red** coat **blue** instead!" he said sternly. "Now go and fetch your coaches."

James was cross. "A splendid red engine like me shouldn't have to fetch his own coaches," he grumbled.

James steamed away too fast with the coaches **groaning** and **moaning** behind. It was a very **bumpy** journey.

James puffed his hardest, but found himself going **slower** and **slower** until they had to stop.

The Driver got out. "All that bumping has made your pipe leak!" he told James.

The passengers and crew had to get off the train.

"We need your bootlace," James' Guard told a passenger. So the man gave his bootlace to the Guard.

Then the Driver put newspaper round the hole to stop the leak and tied it in place with the bootlace.

At last James could set off again. But he knew he was in **BIG trouble** this time.

The Fat Controller sent James to the Sheds in disgrace. James had to stay there **all by himself**. He felt very sad.

Then one morning, The Fat Controller came to see James. "I see you are sorry," he said. "You may pull trucks again."

James beamed from funnel to footplate! **"Thank you, Sir!"** he smiled.

Charlie brought James his train of trucks. "Don't forget your bootlaces, James!" he called cheekily.

The Troublesome Trucks were not happy to see James. "Not you!" they moaned.

James took no notice. He puffed carefully out of the Yard with the trucks **screaming** and **screeching** behind.

Soon James reached a big hill. "It's *ever* so steep," he panted.

Then halfway up, ten naughty trucks broke away and rolled back down again! James had to go back and collect them.

"I can do it, I can do it!" James puffed, as he reached the top of the hill at last.

When James got back to the station, The Fat Controller was very happy.

"You've made the most Troublesome Trucks on the line behave," he smiled. "You may keep your **red paint!**"

"PEEP! PEEP! Hooray!" James whistled. He knew now that he was going to enjoy working on The Fat Controller's Railway.

More about James

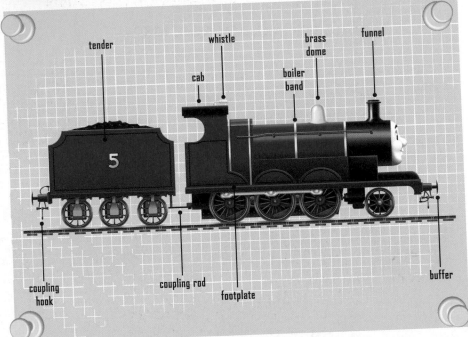

tender

whistle

cab

brass dome

boiler band

funnel

5

coupling hook

coupling rod

footplate

buffer

James' challenge to you

Look back through the pages of this book
and see if you can spot:

sheep

Driver

cow

gull

signals

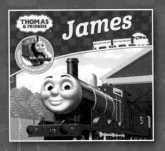
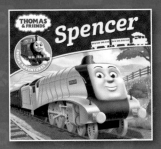
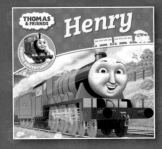
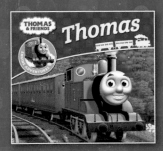